"*A Mossy Story* is a mythological, fantastical short story full of subtle insinuations, symbolism, and analogy; vivid descriptions of scenes and yet room to supplement details with one's own imagination. Strong emotions accompanied my reading of the tale; I felt exquisite pain and yet breathtaking hope at the same time. A reader could peruse this story repeatedly and seize fresh nuances each time."

—MEGAN WARNER
President, Keystone Appraisals

"The writing in *A Mossy Story* truly sings. It exhibits some of the best characteristics modeled by Lewis and Tolkien in that the story is simple and engaging enough to enchant children while also containing a depth of thought that compels adult readers to ponder important questions about life and love. *A Mossy Story* is a great story for parents and children to read and reread together."

—CHRISTIAN DASHIELL
Editorial Fellow, Fatherly

"Readers of all ages will find comfort in Mossy's journey, for it reflects the search of the whole community for purpose and connection to the world around them. Anderson's lyrical prose underscores the mythic and spiritual journey of Mossy, the community, and the land they inhabit, reminding us all that we are part of something larger than ourselves."

—FELICIA SQUIRES
Associate Provost and Dean of Faculty, Corban University

# A Mossy Story

# A Mossy Story

IAN M. ANDERSON

RESOURCE *Publications* · Eugene, Oregon

A MOSSY STORY

Resource Publications
An Imprint of Wipf and Stock Publishers
199 W. 8th Ave., Suite 3
Eugene, OR 97401

www.wipfandstock.com

PAPERBACK ISBN: 978-1-6667-1036-6
HARDCOVER ISBN: 978-1-6667-1037-3
EBOOK ISBN: 978-1-6667-1038-0

VERSION NUMBER 123021

for Alison
There are ball gloves behind your chair and building blocks
on the cushion for the window seat. And now, this little book
upon your lap, my love—boy-mom extraordinaire!


and for P, M, & R
Boys, this small story is yours. It was yours the first time I
whispered Mossy's name to you years ago, and it is yours now.
I pray it will be a signpost for you, a reminder of your place in
God's everlasting kingdom.

# Contents

# Acknowledgments

Thank you to all at Wipf and Stock for taking on this book. It's an honor to partner with you.

Mom and Dad, thank you for reading to me. On the lawn, in the den, at the beach, on the roof. Thank you for showing me how to love writing—I've come a long way since "I hate my journal." When I think back carefully, I can trace the roots of my desire to tell stories to when you first read aloud Aslan's name, but without your further help I wouldn't be typing this now. Thank you.

Alison, thank you for reading this book line by painstaking line, but also thank you for this adventure we've been on! Books are good, and they're better when we share them, but sharing boys is best. May we continue to seek God's wisdom as our sons grow.

P, M, & R, the idea for this book may have started with that horse-dream I had years before your births, but it is because of your very lives that this story means anything. I am thankful for you.

# CHAPTER 1

## An Adventure Begins

In a small town, on a quiet street, sat a square house that was too close-fitting: A full tour of both bedrooms, bathroom, living room, and kitchen took but 23 steps. The family of five that had recently taken residence noticed all the close-fittedness immediately. One might say they lived on top of one another, and they often said so themselves. What else was it they said? Oh, yes, it was that they felt arranged like so many toy blocks neatly lined and stacked in a carrying case.

And so, in a long-feeling couple of months, it became clear to the husband and father that what they all needed—and especially the three young boys—was an adventure. Living, however, on a peaceful street in a peaceful town, such adventures were rare. There was no hope in finding a lurking dragon in a lair or a sneaking spy around a corner; there was no sense in setting off for underground caverns or towers that touch the clouds. Because of this, he decided one night in particular that he would invite his boys into a story, which, as you know, can be a worthy substitute for actual excitements when needed.

As on any other night, the boys bounced off the walls until they were bathed and put to bed. It was when the three young ones wriggled under their sheets that the adventure story begged to be put to work with its enchantment.

So, with delight welling up within his heart, their father whispered to them:

"Do you know about the boy named Mossy?"

Stillness spread over their limbs, and their ears opened. "No," they answered.

Inwardly, their father smiled, for he knew the spell that had been at work upon him for so long had now begun on his sons.

He began the tale this way:

Mossy lived long ago, and he was born the prince of the island kingdom named Cab Nilres. His father and mother ruled well for many years, but the joy they shared in their people and their throne was like a shadow once he was born—yes, and they wondered at how quickly they forgot he was not always with them.

Many wonderful things happened upon Cab Nilres because of Mossy, but the first happened to his father the king. Days had gone by after the boy's birth, and still his name was not yet given to him. It was a source of anguish for his father especially; he knew his deeds were to be great, and therefore his name should be great as well. The servants of the court assumed the child would be named after the king himself or any of a long line of mighty noblemen of the island.

"Not so!" The king roared when he heard these things whispered in his son's presence. "This will not be so!"

All of the court was puzzled at the sudden outburst of the king, but the wisdom of his wife sought him out. She bade him look at her as she held the sleeping child, and she said, "Your son will be named, my husband. I remember of old how the names of great princes were found—and you know the tales well. Go out as your fathers did; go out and search for your son's name. My prayers are always with you." And her words were both peace and salve to his heart.

Immediately the king prepared for his journey into the mountains. He intended to leave the same day his queen's words fell upon his ears even though evening approached and dark clouds hung over the island's mountain peaks.

First upon the back of a sturdy horse, then upon his own two feet, the king climbed into the night. No star showed the way, for he entered the darkness of the clouds as he knew he must. On and on he wound his way up, always speaking aloud his prayers for the name. Drenched and weighed down, he finally slept in the midst of a gathering storm.

Until the sunlight kissed his brow he slept a dreamless sleep, and when he woke, these words poured from his mouth: "Now bestow upon me the name of my son—the prince and future king of Cab Nilres!"

It was then that his eyes were truly opened, for he saw that he lay upon the utmost peak of Mount Clarus. There, glistening in the morning light, grew an ancient, twisted tree. He knew it must have endured storms untold for years unreckoned. And its beauty was such that the king fancied it the wise sage of all trees of the island. "If such a thing is so with the kingdom of the trees," he said, "this one watches over and guards them all."

As soon as the words left his lips, he was struck at the sight of what grew all around and even on the trunk of the tree. He lay there all morning, still like the light on the horizon, for the idea that crept into him was strange. Finally, as the sun rose to its zenith, he spoke the words that grew hot within him. "This humble name shown to me will be given to my son. I looked for might and glory to bestow upon my child, and yet this lowly thing is surely more true—and I know this: from what is humble in human eyes will come what is raised not by human hands."

And in the days after this, when the king refreshed himself in his own court, all his servants wondered at the tale of their lord. "How could such a name befit a prince?" They asked. But the king trusted in the word given to him, and he immediately pronounced his child's name: "He is Mossy!" And though it was a mystery to the court, there was joy at the naming, and the fastest riders of the island brought the news to every coastline so all might rejoice.

These are the days and adventures that followed, yes, that were given to Mossy of Cab Nilres:

When Mossy was three years old, he would stand outside in his parents' garden and look up at the waving branches. First, he stood as still as he could, closed his eyes as the wind blew, and then tried to sway like he saw them sway: back and forth, back and forth, their sounds like a calm tide washing up on the shore. His heart brimming, he would make his way slowly back to his room, and those nights were then full of tree-top dreams.

When Mossy was six, he would scale the tall garden wall and rest his arms and chin on the stone top. From there he could see the sloping valley of willows, aspens, and cottonwoods that led to the sea—the glowing emerald sea. The forest-covered valley seemed to take its form for the purpose of showing the way to the unnamed oceans beyond. He wondered at their pointing arms and beckoning fingers, and he looked until his head ached.

When Mossy was eight, his parents allowed him to explore beyond the garden gate alone, even at night. It was when the wheeling heavens glowed—and the snow crunched, and his breath steamed—that he would stand under the bareness of the trees and ponder whether they spoke of the stars above. It was this year he grew closer to understanding the language of the roots and stems—the ways of roots in the ground and stems in the air meaning more to him than their simple presence. Perhaps, he thought, they told their own tales and talked their own talk. However, as he tried to tell or write down what they meant, the words he chose never fit what the ancient ones had placed within him.

And yet, for all he knew of what lay beyond the garden, his father's castle lured him back with its own curiosities. Eight years had not given him time enough to explore the whole of it, and great halls with great fires welcomed and fed him. Adventures within—from listening to tales spun by his father's men, to hiding in attics and spinning his own tales from the wind that shook the eaves—they, too, grew his taste for wonder.

One such story he heard for the first time that year, one he would carry with him the rest of his days, was told by the island's mightiest knight, Sir Miles. It was of a long lost kingdom of old—even more, of its end. The fires of the hall quieted themselves to hear it, and all those present remained still.

Sir Miles opened his mouth with reluctance, but clearly so none misunderstood. "Across the ocean and through dense forests, a king both good and kind fought against an evil enemy. Pressed, diminished, and wounded, he took his men to himself and bid them retreat. He spoke of one final fortress they may find refuge in, a hidden place within the rocks of a nearby mountain range. They stole away on a moonless night, their king with them. Many times he begged them to go ahead, to find shelter, for he slowed the company due to his wounds. But they refused to leave him.

"As the sun rose, the knights saw their foes had followed to snuff them out, malcontent as they were to take an empty castle. The safety of the rocks ahead was close, but the swift enemy came too fast. The king's men turned, and without a word prepared themselves to charge and stall the attack. In their turn, they begged the king to find a hiding place.

"But the king's eyes flamed. His bleeding wounds forgotten, he sat straight upon his steed and meant his last command to be obeyed. To the end he and they were one.

"And the charge began their final battle. The love they bore for one another drove them on, and though they scattered the evil foe, together all paid for victory with his last breath."

For long moments, a hush remained upon the hall-fires as well as upon the hearers, and none spoke until Sir Miles raised his wine and drank to the health of his men.

As was told, Mossy carried this tale for all his life, and he held it close for the sorrow of it and the mystery of the charge he pictured in his imagination—it was a mystery because he knew their end, and even so, he hoped at each new hearing for the salvation of them all. And what was the glint in Sir Miles's eye? Was it sorrow? Mossy pondered these things, and the story took on for him new meanings as he learned more of the island and more of his place in it.

Another tale at work on Mossy came from his tutor, and he received it once a year from before he knew a world existed outside the garden wall. The two of them would sit within the cover of the willow tree that grew in the inner courtyard of the castle, and as the stars rolled into view, the myth of the island rolled off the Old One's tongue.

"The whole of this grand isle we call Cab Nilres was volcanic mountains; the peaks grumbled and spewed so nothing grew upon the ground, and Man avoided its shores to its shame and further eruptions. That is, until the first of our kind, one expelled from his homeland for speaking truth to corrupt kings, was guided by God's hand to the black shore.

"With no other choice before him—for his small vessel was broken to pieces by storm and rock—he braved the flowing lava and sought after the upset depths. Many times the fire-rivers trapped him, and he could but sit and pray for the peace of the isle, for its troubles and curses to end. If not for his prayers, the island would have split into two, for lightning from heaven battered it, and its own rage furthered the curse. This is why the canyon that runs like a deep wound from north to south across Cab Nilres is a reminder to all of the island's curse and sorrow. Because these things are so, no man or woman crosses the canyon without a shudder and a prayer for mercy.

"But all was not lost, and this First One was given images of times to come. Times of refreshment for the desolate island, but also a time of distress."

Here, Mossy's tutor always stopped, and Mossy would ask, "Dear Tutor, why do you never tell the rest? Why do you always hold back?"

"The time is not yet for you to hear," was the old, familiar reply, and on with more mild studies they went, on with histories and ancient names, or manners and court news, the origin of Cab Nilres always slow to fade away from the young boy's mind.

When Mossy was twelve—and looking forward to his thirteenth birthday with anxious excitement—his tutor could no longer hold him off with the partial history of Cab Nilres, but knew he had to speak of its troubles to come. And this is how he continued the tale:

"The First One rejoiced in what he saw at the beginning of the isle's refreshment: the greening of the ground, which was the birth of the forest you know so well. But as he watched from where he stood on the highest mountain, he beheld a future blackness from across the sea, one that swept up the beautiful shores and threatened the kingdom that had grown so strong."

Mossy interrupted. "Is this the prophecy of what's to come? Of my father's kingdom?" His tutor made as if to reply, but then bowed his head and remained silent. "Some men whisper of it only in the light of day, and others laugh at what they call nursery talk. What of them?"

The tutor, who of a sudden looked to Mossy to be an ancient man, replied, "I speak what I know." A moment passed and a flickering spear-like light grew in his eyes. He continued, "And your father's men would do well to hear and know rightly."

Mossy sat, his tutor's words and look turning his heart over. He opened his mouth to ask a question in order to change the subject, and yet he knew he could keep his secret no longer; he had not kept anything from his tutor, neither fear nor desire, and he avoided the temptation to do so now. Mossy told his tutor of a frightening dream that had come to him, a dream of jet black chargers galloping toward him. His voice cracked as he went on. "The ground shook, and they searched for my face. As suddenly as they came toward me, all was stilled. And I stood under the stars before the horde, their breath rising grey upon the black, the sound of waves breaking at my back."

They sat in silence for long moments that lay heavy upon them both. "What might it mean, Tutor?"

The old man's look softened before his student's fears, and he reassured him. "Be at peace, Mossy. It is a dream you will have many more times, and soon you will come to desire instead of fear it."

Mossy took a deep breath, and the easy swish of the willow branches spread a new calm upon him. The hand of his tutor rested on his shoulder, and he heard this further word, "A grave deed is in store, but by and by you will know of the hope of this isle."

Long after his tutor had gone, Mossy sat under the tree with thoughts of his dream, time passed, and time to come swaying through him. He hung on his tutor's words and let them work on the live images in his mind, but days were coming when Mossy's faithfulness would be tested.

Months after this, it was time to prepare for service in his father's guard. Days and nights spent with his tutor were replaced with training for war. He joined noblemen's sons of the same age, all of whom knew what their next birthday would bring: The Week of Knights. Each father would invite his son to the tent set up to represent their family, and each tent was part of a mighty gathering. Banners and standards, their colors bright against the sky, would wave and snap on the wind.

But what Mossy and the other boys longed for more than banners and games of war came on the last day of the encampment. All were to leave behind their weapons and fight in hand-to-hand combat; one by one the knights would enter the middle of the ring surrounded with shield-bearers and call his son. From the opposite end his boy would enter and accept the terms: defeat his father and exit with him, or suffer defeat and return to his place among boys.

It was always a week that began with the highest spirits. Contests of strength roared on, the smell of rare game from long hunts floated through the air, and fires burned deep into the night as men of valor told tales in the midst of their peers and sons.

As the final day approached, however, the camp would grow quiet, for the knowledge of battles to come focused and sharpened their nerves.

So it was with Mossy as he made himself ready, and yet, adventures were to come—adventures his heart ached for, but his head knew not.

Mossy woke in the middle of the night from the recurring dream of horses charging to meet him on the starlit beach. At first he tried to ignore the strange thoughts that kept him awake, yet the glow of horse eyes haunted him, and the wind also did its best to howl and drive sleep far from him. Finally, he stoked the fire outside his father's tent, wrapped his outdoor garments around his shoulders, and gave his full attention to the night sounds and the tugging on his mind the dream produced.

Before him, the logs he put in the flames popped and crackled merrily, and his feet were warmed. Yet it was the treetops that Mossy's ears sought to hear. Now they bent in a gust of wind, now they swayed easily in a softer breeze. The more he sat and listened, the more he imagined wild stretches of forest—the crowns of massive, ancient trees bent toward him and then thrown back. He was so filled that all sense of time left him, and when his fire burned low again, when all that remained of each log was a glowing coal, his cold legs shook him from his waking dream.

The sun was only the hope of the eastern horizon, and moonlight splashed over the island. Mossy walked back toward his father's castle, his heart a drumbeat of a desire he couldn't name. With the thump of his chest in his ears, and the full silver moon feeding him, he entered the open courtyard, which was empty but for shadows, and continued quickly inside.

He waded through the soft grey light in the great halls on his way to the garden he used to delight in, but all the while he thought of the misgiving feeling that grew inside. At last he stood in the middle of the garden, his hands stretched out in front of him as if to ask for help. His breath smoked before him, clouding the young, tremulous leaves and hiding for a moment the pale stars. And as if to answer his plea, the door in the garden wall unlatched and opened so the wind could just sneak in and flow past him. It was not odd to him then that the gale once again tried to rip the crowns of all the trees from their tops; it lifted his hair and forced his eyes closed, and for a brief and joyful time he forgot himself in the rush of air.

As suddenly as it had begun, the wind ceased. Mossy heard himself laughing, and his outstretched hands became uplifted branches swaying back and forth, back and forth. Soon, however, he was still and saw the garden door, which was now wide open.

He moved quickly to exit through the wall and enter the forest, his heart ringing in his ears once more.

The moonbeams traced his path so his way opened before him through the night, for the moon hung low on the horizon. Once he could no longer see the castle walls, he stopped and saw how far he had come. Silver light danced in the trees, and the trunks seemed to be cast in precious metal on one side and were a mystery of shadows on the other. Branches creaked and moaned; a burst of wind sent last year's decayed leaves flying. Mossy sat and leaned his head on a rock and listened. He searched the night sounds for what brought him away from the camp, and he tried to feel again what had been so clear when the garden door opened.

It was then that these words pierced the air: "You won't find yourself able to remake within you what came to you outside your will." Mossy scrambled to his feet and turned toward the speaker. A tall but bent figure in a hooded gown stood illuminated by the soft light behind Mossy. "Fear not. You know me, Mossy, though you've begun to forget. Tonight you have a choice before you, and I am here to take you to the place of your choosing."

"How do I know you are worthy of my trust?" Mossy asked.

"I know the dream that woke you, the one that haunts you time and time again. And I watched as you delighted in the wind and in the trees this very night—as you did as a child."

Mossy trembled at the reply but did not think to run. The hooded figure held out an ancient hand and said, "Do you know me?"

Without answering the question, Mossy said, "Where will you take me?"

"Come and see."

The hand remained outstretched, and Mossy asked, "And what is the choice?"

But the reply was again, "Come and see."

Even though he trembled anew as he walked toward his guide, Mossy's resolve grew strong, and he took the hand given to him.

"I am Lord Salix. You are the future king of Cab Nilres. Tonight you must decide what sort of king you will be. Let us go—the night will not wait."

Through the last of late hours, Lord Salix and Mossy rushed up and up the slopes of the forest. At each fork of their way they always took the hard, rocky, steep path, and Mossy's legs and mind became weary.

Finally, on the crest of a hill that overlooked a small valley, Lord Salix stopped and faced Mossy.

"Hold your head up, Small One." At the words, Mossy tried to catch his breath and obey. "Stand so I can support you. The air will return to your lungs, and you must see clearly."

Against Lord Salix's side, Mossy rested until he could stand on his own.

"Look out and down on this secret valley. What do you see?"

"The dark shapes of trees," Mossy said. "Black masses of growing shadows, and—" he strained to see and fought the urge to blink, but in the end looked away.

"And?" It was a soft, expectant question.

Mossy replied, "And a small light."

"Perhaps you think you dreamed or hoped for light amidst so much darkness."

Mossy did not speak.

"You saw truly. Look for it again."

And so he lifted his head and looked.

"The last of the night's stars shine on a lake. This is the small light. I will take you there—if you choose to go." A quiet moment passed, and Lord Salix continued, "Now, look down the way we came. When the sun shines on the castle wall this morning, your servants will find you in your tent if you turn back now. This night will soon be like a dream—if you so choose."

"Is it all a dream then, this flight through the wood?"

"Is the time we spent under the willow a dream to you now?" Lord Salix removed his hood and smiled.

Mossy's heart leapt at the familiar face. "Tutor!"

"It is so. But even now you must decide. Turn back, join the other boys and knights in their gathering, and forget this night in time. Or come with me, see what waits for you, and save the isle from advancing peril."

"But will the island not be saved if I return to bring word of trouble?"

"That knowledge is not mine. It may be so; it may not."

Mossy thought of too much all at once—The Week of Knights, the games, the fights, his father—all he had begun to long for—

"Time passes, Mossy."

And below, in the valley, when he looked upon it, he heard the wind as it had blown in the trees at the first of the night, how his whole being had ached to know what this longing and call was, and why it came to him.

"Mossy?"

"Tutor—my lord," Mossy said, "I am split in two." A new tear ran down his cheek as he continued, "But take me down into the valley. I will follow you."

And on they rushed.

# CHAPTER 2

# King, Kingdom, and the Black Flags

Listen, as the tale continues, for this is how we find things on the island of Cab Nilres after the night Mossy and Lord Salix ran into the unknown:

Mossy had gone, to return in time, and the kingdom mourned him. When Father King and Mother Queen should be making all ready for their son to be received in The Week of Knights, instead they heard news of his disappearance. Furthermore, as they sat in court waiting for tidings of Mossy, scouts from the shores appeared—worry of their own on their brows.

"Please," said the king, "what message do you carry?"

At this, the chief scout came near, but knew what he must speak would add to his lord and lady's burden, not lift it. He bowed and spoke. "Lord, Lady, we bring our burdens to you, as the kingdom bears little of what you bear. Forgive my dark news to come. Ship after ship this season, full of men seeking safe harbor, have fear in their bones and tidings of black war galleons that fly black flags."

All the court waited for the king's reply, but none came. He looked at the messenger, yet seemed to see through him.

"My lord, each merchant vessel reports the slow but sure advance of these black-flagged ships upon your kingdom."

As a thick curtain falls heavily upon the stage, another silence fell on all who heard. No one dared to speak, but they looked toward their lord and hoped for his command. However, the king only said, "Say on."

"These men who know the sea are hearty men, kin to warriors, and hardened through trials. They have filled the port villages, and their word from ship to ship is the same. Some were close enough to see their motionless features—men with pale white faces and cold eyes, men who—"

"Then to Cab Nilres they come indeed." Sir Miles, the knight always at the king's side, spoke his interruption, then said to his lord, "Command it, my lord, and we will begin the call for the island to retreat here and your armed men to advance to the shore."

Before an answer could be made, another messenger entered in haste. His hair was windblown and his countenance told of his fear. He rushed toward the thrones with all speed and said, "Forgive my bold approach, my lord, my lady, but my errand bids me forget fine courtesy." The young man bowed and continued, "This morning, from the tower on the easternmost point, word arrived that with the rising of the sun came hateful shadows on the waters. Even as your faithful servants watched, the shadows spread and became an armada both dark and massive. Ships of war, my lord. They come."

The knight asked, "And what of the other coastal watchtowers?"

"Their fires were lit hours ago, to send warning. I passed many fleeing crowds of your people along my way here."

The goodly knight gripped his sword as he turned away from the messenger to the king. He knelt before the throne, and, with head bowed, said, "You must command it, my king. The bridge must be fortified." When still no reply came, he choked back sudden tears and whispered so only the king and queen heard, "My lord, what is your will?"

But the king did not stir, even at the touch of the queen. The court then saw his lips move without sound; Sir Miles rose and bent his ear to listen. Quickly afterward, the knight's voice boomed. "Go to! Send word to all watchtowers! Make ready the bridge to receive those who live below the river-canyon! Send wagons for those who cannot ride! Give way to any scout with further news!" And as quickly as these things were spoken, the court emptied of all but king, queen, and personal attendants.

In the quiet that followed, the stones of the castle's courtroom groaned and longed to cry out for the island and its people, but also for the king and queen because their grief was double.

Finally, the queen said, "What bodes on your mind weighs on mine as well." She reached for the hand of her husband and sought to look into his eyes. "And yet I will hope with you that until a final word about Mossy falls upon my ears, despair will not rule us. He will return."

At her soft words, the king's heart moved within him, and his tears were great. "Before word of war filled this place, before our hands were forced to action by this unknown darkness, I feared for Mossy. And now—now his absence is a greater burden, and worry overtakes me so I cannot think to save our isle." He searched the queen's face, and his brows furrowed all the more as he asked, "How shall this cloud be lifted?"

His wife answered, "Your faithful servant Sir Miles has seen your sorrow. Know that he has therefore moved on your behalf. Your men make ready to fight—"

But he interrupted, "And of Mossy?" His question struck her, for she sought to cover her pain with words of battle. King and queen looked upon one another, unspoken fear swimming in their minds.

A horn in the hall broke their silence, and a new messenger, an old man of a sturdy build, walked toward them. He bowed and waited for the blessing to speak.

"Please," said the king. "What word?"

"My lord, my lady." He raised his head, and as he did so, a new pang pulled at them. "My news is of a strange nature, and I fight within my own mind even now whether to give it. Yet I know I must. I've dreamed of The Week of Knights, my lord."

The king smiled reluctantly and said, "As have all the boys of an age. What of it?"

"As you say, my lord. But this dream—it has come upon me night after night. I thought to let it pass, but all the more it came. The more I dreamed, the more clearly I saw. It is your face that I dreamed of, and it is refreshed as I look on you now. I saw you standing ready to receive your son—"

"No more!" It was the queen's voice that silenced the messenger, and he bowed at her command. She watched her husband's tears fall as the messenger spoke, and she could not bear them.

"Please, my lady," the old man spoke though he still bowed his head. "I have traveled far, from the far side of Mount Clarus, and my inmost being bids me—nay, urges me—to say on. The more news I heard as I made my way, the more I have become convinced of my message's import. And I do but speak what I must: do not allow such evil to halt The Week of Knights. Forgive my impudent talk. And yet—The Week must go on."

"Why must it go on?" The king's question rang and echoed off the walls to the ears of those present, and all felt his urgency.

"I know not, my lord. But I saw your son, too. He will return. Have faith." At this last word the old man stood straight and said, "Please forgive my unseemly ways."

"They need not be forgiven," the king replied, and he rose and walked toward the messenger. He took his hand and said, "A strange dream, yes, but a welcome word." A smile spread over the king's face, and he swallowed hard. Looking at the old man, he spoke a command to his nearest servant, "Warm, new clothes, a spiced drink, meat—" and to the dreamer, "stay with us so we may show hospitality. You look weary. My servants will show you the way."

With another bow, the man departed, his countenance eased by the kindness shown to him.

The king met his wife's gaze, and it was his turn to watch her tears fall. She reached for his hand, and they embraced. Finally, the king spoke.

"It will be so," the king said to the last of his servants. "Let plans for The Week of Knights go forth. Let no enemy take our joy." His sure command spurred his servants to work, and their strength was renewed at his resolve.

One spoke, "My lord, as Sir Miles moves about and makes ready for battle, the valley which hosts The Week fills with your people. Even now, from your throne room windows, I see many who have fled the coming strife. There will be no room, my lord."

"Show me." The king stepped to the nearby window and saw what had been said was true. Many new campfires sent smoke into the air from the site of The Week of Knights. "You say well, my lad. And this is what I say: invite them all—it will be a Week unlike any before it."

The rest of his servants departed at his word, their hearts heavy for their king, for they hoped against the ill tidings that all would be as the dreamer spoke and their lord desired.

In the same way, the king and queen laid up hope that the dream was a true one, and neither dared to speak contrary to it, so great was their desire for it to come to pass.

So the people of the isle drew near to the castle. Some traveled from the farthest eastern shores, some from nearby woods, but all found aid from the king's advancing knights. Many an old man and many a mother lifted their hands to bless and offer a prayer for their defenders, for the battle to come drew near.

The castle sat high on the tallest mountain of Cab Nilres, with sheer cliffs to guard its rear to the west and north. A canyon ran through the middle of the island north to south and cut off all roads save the ancient stone bridge.

Because of this canyon, all who lived on the eastern side of the isle had to travel along its way toward the bridge to cross to further safety. For days to come it would be crowded both with common folk and knights. Its defense was made ready in due time, prepared as a last line against the advancing foe.

# CHAPTER 3

## A Night Council

Though we long to know what shall become of the invasion of Cab Nilres, we must go back to the night before the king and queen received the ill news of the enemy, back to Mossy and his travels with Lord Salix. They rushed on into a secret valley when we left them, and now you will hear what they found next.

It felt to Mossy that they flew through the trees endlessly, and hot was the fire that burned within him. However, as the branches swept by, some brushed his cheeks, and others whizzed overhead, leaving night-scents on his brow that cooled him. This was a great kindness shown to him, for every moment rushed him farther away from his home, from all he knew, and from the desire of his youth.

And yet it was not long before he and Lord Salix stood near the shore of the hidden lake. Indeed, as his breath rose before him, and at intervals clouded the reflection of the stars on the water, he was like one who had been there always, like one who had forever known the glistening of these stars upon the peace of this water.

"Make yourself still, Mossy," said Lord Salix, "and keep your eyes open."

Mossy tried to slow his breathing and focused his attention on the faint ripples just yards below.

"We are not alone. Soon you will see."

A great crack shattered the silence around them, and Mossy looked for what made the sound. More noises like the first, but farther away, shot toward them and the ground trembled.

"Stand sure, Mossy. A long-held desire of your child-days is granted you this night." Lord Salix reached out and steadied Mossy's shoulder. At his ear, Lord Salix's hand popped, creaked, and then released its hold. Mossy turned his head and watched his tutor's fingers stretch into thin, thread-like branches. His heart pounded in his chest as though to break out.

"Mossy, do not fear." Lord Salix smiled upon Mossy. "Frightened child, do not fear, but stand and listen." At the words, Lord Salix's form bent and grew over Mossy's head, all the while crackling and snapping.

Mossy prayed for all sounds and trembling to cease, but both intensified so he thought he was lost. He fell to his knees, and panic overtook him—he swooned and fainted.

The old dream of horses emerging from unfathomed depths followed as soon as he hit the ground, and the breath of the beasts he stood among mixed with his own. Quickly, the scene flashed and changed, and immediately he rode one of the massive, angry horses as it charged first over solid turf, and then leapt and rode upon the air. Mossy screamed.

Upon waking, he scrambled to his feet and would have run, but soon realized he was under a familiar willow tree. He smiled and choked on his relief, saying aloud as he wiped tears from his face, "How the dream changed! What can it mean? I quake within! But what comfort you are, willow." He leaned on the trunk and let the sweep of the branches soothe his terror away. Indeed, the cover of the tree and its way in the wind reassured him as the willow within the castle courtyard had so often done. For a moment, Mossy thought he was at home. However, another sound met his ears, and the memory of the night's events returned like no dream, for he heard the soft lap of lake water on the nearby shore.

Mossy forced himself to look. Now clinging to the trunk, he tried to see what he had heard. As he searched in vain for an opening in the willow, the branches separated and held themselves apart—and he knew what it meant; he was to pass through.

"Lord Salix?" Mossy's voice was small, and his question died on the night air. "Tutor?" He knew he must pass through the parted branches, but his feet felt like stones. He stayed a second more in the willow's shelter, and the branches, which rustled in the same breeze that kissed the lake's surface, whispered their peace to him.

"Stand sure, Mossy." Lord Salix's words came back to him. He took a deep breath and passed through his only refuge.

What he found instead of the shoreline of the lake was the thickest stand of trees he had ever seen. He could hear the water, but the closeness of the trunks kept him from seeing it.

"Please. I don't understand." Mossy pressed his hands on the nearest cottonwoods, their deep trunk-ruts a fitting resting place for his fingers. Again, a mighty crack split the cold air. Mossy flinched and thought to hide once more within the willow, but for wonder's sake he was still. An avenue opened as he watched; roots swam in earth, branches danced in a great living latticework—and again Mossy saw the lake. His hands traced the way from trunk to trunk until the water lapped at his feet.

"Mossy." Behind him a voice spoke, and it was like the mild clap of aspen leaves to his overwhelmed mind.

He turned and beheld a tall woman dressed in a long gown and garland that fell over her shoulders; where the garland ended and gown began, Mossy couldn't tell, and it all quivered in the breeze so whether she spoke or remained silent, the sound of murmuring leaves was constant.

"Mossy, take my hand." She beamed at him as she said this, and her clothes smelled like a long-awaited spring.

Trembling, Mossy reached out and took her hand.

"We mean you no harm. On the contrary, we are glad to finally make a formal greeting."

"If you please, I only see you, Lady."

"Then turn and look."

A chill crept up his spine and covered his scalp at the thought of the trees behind him. He remembered for a moment the wisps of willow limbs that had been his tutor's hair, and he wanted instead to keep his gaze on the lady and the open expanse of the lake.

"Mossy," the lady entreated him, knowing his heart. "Do not fear. You will learn to be among us. Turn and see who greets you."

Without releasing the lady's hand, Mossy did as she bade him do. He turned and looked back up the slope and lost his breath at the sight. Instead of the close-standing trees, he beheld a company of men and women—though he knew they were something other than the men or women of his father's kingdom. Some wore robes that were the silvery grey of buds wrapped tightly against the winter; others looked more like their earlier forms and wore leaves, as did the lady on the shore, or bark in the place of skin. And even though they appeared to stand motionless if looked at one by one, the whole swayed with the wind—blade-like leaves and thin stems clicking their music in step.

"But I do fear," said Mossy.

"Do not look away, small son of Adam; the host that came to you parts again."

And Mossy saw this: Slowly, a way was made so he could see the weeping willow. Its boughs hung over onto the ground, and Mossy felt tears build up behind his eyes. A question he had never thought to ask came to his lips, and he said, "Lady, why does the willow weep?" A tear fell from his cheek, and he asked, "Why does Lord Salix weep?"

"Boy," said the lady, "this is the first reason you've been called. You must know."

The trees-turned-men and -women bowed toward Lord Salix, and as he watched, the willow itself swept lower than before, twisted, and with a great moan and shuddering of stems once more became the tutor of days gone by. Soon, Lord Salix walked down the aisle of trees, receiving their gestures of honor with a nod, and stood before Mossy.

"The boy asks why you weep, my lord," said the lady, and Mossy heard a new breeze give life to her garment of leaves.

"Then he is truly ready." Lord Salix looked upon Mossy and continued, "Tonight, the heavens wait to give you the dream of this island called Cab Nilres. Will you accept it?"

Mossy swallowed away the pain in his throat and answered, "I will."

"Even as you dream, remember our time together. Remember the story we've shared, the story of your home—of our home. Your place in that story is being fashioned. Remember these things, Mossy." Lord Salix paused and smiled kindly. Finally, he said, "When you wake, you will be alone."

Before Mossy could ask another question, the stars swirled into ribbons of white and spun themselves upon him; he fell to the ground with his hands to his face.

It was when he could take no more that he heard the familiar voice of his tutor, and his ears tingled at the words. "These around you tonight are my brothers, my sisters, my cousins. We have all waited for you, Mossy, but I have waited from before this isle was anything but a curse. It was I who first received these words:

> When a son of man goes between:
> Link of Earth to Man, like link of Tree to Earth,
> Then will the very rocks cry out
> To vanquish a great and terrible Evil.

And:

> The word of his mouth
> Brings forth healing.

And again:

> His throne will become great
> Upon the isle of Cab Nilres.

"For generations, Mossy, we sought one like you. Now, receive a fuller understanding."

A warm hand pressed down on Mossy's head, and he slept. In his dreaming he had three visions:

Immediately many waters rushed together in white foam and roaring green waves. From unseen depths a mountain emerged with spouts of fire and billows of steam. As it grew, Mossy knew what he saw—his island home in its birth.

Peace settled upon the new rock, and all seemed good to him. Soon, however, masses of black clouds gathered all around, and lightning flashed until it beat upon the peaks of Cab Nilres. The response was a burning sulfur, putrid and suffocating to all that had begun to grow, until the isle turned black. And still the rocks split, and the peaks roared in their fountains of flame.

Mossy bowed his head; his cheeks burned from the shame of what he witnessed, for he knew that the anger of the isle was due to its separation from Mankind—and its curse came from Man's inaction to resist the bent of evil. In this way Mossy remembered his tutor's lessons even while he dreamed.

Rain fell and stemmed the flow of liquid fire that glowed over the isle's surface. And on the shore amidst a wrecked boat, a man crawled to avoid death from both sea and fire.

Through steam and rain and flowing lava this First One sought peace—and again Mossy knew this man and his prayers. The First One stumbled and walked on until, as he turned to mark his way, lightning pierced the tumultuous island and would have split it in two had he not raised his hands to call for mercy. His head bowed, he mixed his tears with rain, and both poured over his arched body as he cried for help and an end to the curse.

And Mossy watched days pass. The storm and the eruptions ceased, yet the man remained bowed with outstretched hands.

A new rain fell, soft and warm. This new blessing fell on both man and island, and bright grass grew. The First One's appearance was altered, too. His hair lengthened, his cloak hardened, his up-lifted arms splintered, and his feet dug into the wet earth. In time, the rain stopped, and the newly-formed willow glistened in the sun.

Mossy turned and watched the whole of the isle spring to life as though the willow itself inspired it to spread toward the neigh-boring peaks and the shores all around. Ships landed; men made their homes; a castle rose around Mossy and his tree. Soon, the dream faded, but there, under the tree, his tutor's presence comforted him.

Immediately, Mossy found himself on the lake's shore where he met the host of the island's trees, but with this difference: he stood alone. The images of his dream stayed with him a moment more, until a sound behind him caused him to turn. It was a small fire of glowing coals popping and settling into itself.

Mossy was grateful, and he walked to it. His hands and feet warmed quickly. The deep orange of the fire reminded him of the anger and shame of the isle, but soon he remembered Lord Salix within the willow, and he smiled. By and by he wanted sleep and made ready to lie down. However, a strong urge to stand and turn toward the lake rose inside him, and he obeyed even in his weariness. He ached after something, and he searched the opposite shore as well as he could from his place by the fire. He saw only black shapes against the grey night and the slight ebb of water.

Gradually, like the change of dawn upon the night sky, a clear beam of light rose and then shot through the wood and across the lake. It flickered and illuminated the whole shore so Mossy had to cover his eyes; quickly the brightness faded and focused to a point.

Mossy's hands and arms trembled when he realized the light approached him. Without warning, the vision changed. Mossy lay face down on the sand, the fire near. Slowly, he looked up and saw the figure of a man walking toward him; the man flashed like lightning. Though Mossy still trembled, a flood of joy welled up inside him.

The man drew close, and again Mossy covered himself because of the brightness. He pressed himself down in the sand, but he could yet sense the constant flashing light, for it was upon him.

"Mossy, rise and see." The voice reminded Mossy of the roar of the high tide, like many waters that crashed upon starlit cliffs.

He obeyed and walked to the man kneeling by the fire of coals, his light somehow bearable now.

"Your lips will be pure by the touch of fire and the touch of my hand, and you will be clean by the flow of the icy lake and my word to you."

The next few moments Mossy fought back terror as he had never known it. The man who glowed like the untouchable light of storms took a red-hot coal from the fire and brought it to him.

"May I touch your lips?"

"I can't bear it," Mossy replied.

"No, you cannot."

Mossy's terror grew at this answer, and he thought for a moment he would run.

"May I touch your lips?"

This time the question bore down on him with a weight that made him bow his head. He finally managed to whisper, "Yes."

The coal burned through Mossy's lips, and he would have fallen from the agony had the man not caught him up in his arms. Soon the soft sounds of water surrounded Mossy's head, and the searing burn ceased.

He awoke alone, these words in the air: "Be new." And the lakeshore received the flow of minute ripples from the silent moonlit center. He thought of the two dreams as the water pulled at his feet; he recalled the tears and prayers of Lord Salix, and the bronze eyes of the one who visited him on the beach. A calm settled on him in the midst of his recollection, and he waited—but for what, he did not know. Even as he turned his thoughts over, a third and final vision came to him.

Though he knew he sat within the secret valley along the water's edge, he beheld his child-days. He stood in the garden, waving with the trees; he climbed the wall and dreamed with the valley of the sea; he wandered alone among the forest. All this was familiar.

And then he beheld a day and night that had escaped his memory. His wandering became instead a search far into dripping groves and steep hollows. He examined branchlets and young limbs that had begun to draw warm sap from within, somehow knowing all the while how the colors would deepen and change the entirety of the island into a vibrant tapestry. It was then, he now remembered, that brown and grey had looked new to him. The colors shook off their dullness and gave him a knowledge of their riches Mossy had not known. He marveled anew.

The forest floor changed from leaf-paths and root-steps to a thick carpet of bright moss—and it changed while he lost himself in his wonder. He looked back to find all the ways around him were so covered.

Fear replaced the awe in his heart, and he could think of no other thing but to sit and clear his head. A fog rose, and the trees dripped and clicked in the new light. A wind spoke over Mossy's face, causing him to press his back against the nearest trunk. It, too, was covered with soft green moss, and it surrounded him as if in an embrace. His breaths slowed, his head drooped, and he slept.

Immediately he thought he fell, and he shook himself. But he did not wake. The fog grew thick so his hair and clothes were soaked. All became wet and soft. In his sleep he was pulled into the moss, into the ground. He no longer feared.

And then he saw, but not with eyes, and heard, but not with ears; he saw the constant flow of the communion of roots, and he heard the throb and drum of the rhythm of the earth. Into networks and patterns—like streams of thought—he fell. He became more aware than ever of things that are above. Bright sun, air, rain clouds, even of creatures perched on branches. His scalp tingled with light, and each hair of his head, like countless turning leaves, reached out to bathe in warmth.

Then all was quiet and dark. A small trickling noise crept around him, and he knew water fell on the ground above. A new rain, he thought, a rain for roots. So it was. He felt the seeping rain on his arms and fingers as the earth channeled it to him—even his brow cooled amidst its touch.

Mossy awoke to his own laughter.

By the secret lake he was alone, and his visions ended.

# CHAPTER 4

# The Hope of Cab Nilres

We've left Mossy on the secret shore as he thinks about his visions and allows their joyful mystery to wash over him. We will return to him and his further deeds, but more must be told of the island—of the forests, of the vast caverns, of the rock of its foundation—for he and the island were bound together from his birth, and although the court of the king gladly awaited the prince's growth into manhood, they were not alone in their expectation.

Listen! As Mossy learned, the people of the island were not the only ones who were stirred to action as he grew from child to man, seemingly, in one night. Those strange ladies and lords who met him on the shore of the secret lake were few compared to all the rest. Long before his father's father was born and given a name, long before men set foot on Cab Nilres, as Lord Salix has told, the whole of the isle ached for healing. And for numberless generations it waited patiently, silently.

The day Mossy's father-king discovered his boy's name atop the mountain peak, he spoke these words, "From what is humble in human eyes will come what is raised not by human hands." In his joy, he did not see or hear the effect of his own words. And yet, anyone who had eyes to see or ears to hear—anyone who had heard the ancient whispers from of old and had not scorned them—saw

and heard and felt for days following his prophecy what was be-
lieved to be impossible.

Those whose homes lay in lonely thickets or in overgrown
stands of the ancient woods spoke of the expectation of the trees.
Hermits who had not walked within the haunts of men for years
upon years came and told what they had seen.

One such reticent soul made his way from the oldest wood
of the isle straight into a public-house, and his fear of the common man melted with the telling of his tale. He stood upon the
threshold while he searched for words, the evening light glowing
lavender behind him, until the merry ones inside hushed and
turned toward him. His face was hidden, for the dying light of day
had turned his whole figure black, and this made their ears all the
more ripe for what he said.

"Hear what I say and be ready! As the sun peaked in the azure
heights today, I gathered sticks among the towers of the forest. No
breeze moved the air. The cottonwood leaves did not stir, and for
that reason I stopped and looked. It was then, as the noonday light
burned on high, that the whole of the wood moved as one."

At this one or two laughed outright, but the teller did not
hesitate to continue, nor did the jeers of their mouths lead him
back into fear.

"It is so—as one the giants shook and their roots crawled as if
to release themselves from bondage. For one moment all was astir
and then was still. I, too, remained still in my terror—but hear this:
It is for the hope of further joy that the trees have moved. It is in
such a hope that I speak. Hear, believe, and make ready!"

The door to the public-house slammed, shutting out the sudden night. A few young men broke the painful silence as they rose
and followed the hermit down starlit paths and into open glens,
so grave was their desire to know more. The others remained
quiet, and the words soaked into their minds. Even those who had
mocked held their tongues. Newly stacked platters of food and
drink came 'round, and yet over the whole night hung the weight
of the mystery they had heard.

In another part of Cab Nilres, far from the then-silent public-house, where the twin peaks Connatus and Gemellus loomed over simple villages of simple people, a great and mighty thing was revealed.

The people of these villages were known for their skill in mining the treasures of the mountains; they smelted rare metals and set precious gems, and their fine wares were found in all corners of the island, even in the courts of the king. They knew the corridors and caverns well—all those twisted and maze-like ways were familiar roads to them, and their love of the mountain revealed a further gift.

Indeed, the very day the hermit of the forest witnessed the singular movement of the trees, many of the humble miners stopped their work to listen to what sounded to them like a song that echoed from depths even they had not explored. It was a melody that resounded and throbbed so each miner ceased his work; those who had worked with flying arms stood listening, their ears afire.

Though they did not move, it felt to them that the music stole them away into the mountains. "The toll of drums that live," so they said afterward, "took us into dreams." And they knew not how long they listened, nor did they know how long they remained once the music ended, for even when it stopped their common desire to hear more held them in their places.

"Do we yet dream?" They asked one another when they finally took the homeward path. "Is it all dream and not true that the mountain's heart called out?" Many were gathered that night among the villages, and they spoke of the same rhythmic sounds that refused to release them. For years to come they told their wide-eyed children, "The mountain sang to our souls with groans inexpressible, and we will forever know the language."

Because of this the miners stand within the caverns and listen before they work, hoping that the day has come when they will hear the music anew—and more!—that the song's meaning will be revealed. As they approach and later depart the mines, this is their greeting and their farewell to one another, "May that Day quickly come!" Faithfully they wait and pray, standing watch for what they yearn to hear.

Open your ears again, for there are yet more whose strange experiences must be told. Others, who lived far from the shadows of the island's mountains, were also called to wait in expectation.

Those who made their homes on the plains of Cab Nilres smiled at the idea that the land had been rolled out like a scroll, for many of the shepherds of the grassland made poetry beside their fires at night, and the wide, almost unending, stretches of the plains hushed them as a poem might hush its listeners.

Is it a surprise, then, that some who led their sheep over the lonely fields upon those plains said wonderful things, things most unbelievable, the same day the forest-hermit proclaimed his news and the simple miners stood entranced by what they heard?

"Today the ground warmed beneath me," one shepherd told his gathered family. Their hearth glowed orange as the fire popped and sent sparks heavenward, and night sounds flowed through the open windows—the swish of long grasses and the call of ground owls just come awake. "The deep earth is always warm, 'tis true," he said. "And yet, the heat came like the rhythm of a spoken song, and in my mind I saw burning embers in a soft wind lit up, then blackened, and lit up again." Silence grew and settled over the little room. Only the fire and the night sounds were unmoved. Soon, however, the children asked for more—like children of all ages will often ask—for they thought their father spoke a poetry like many other nights when he wove such wonders for them all.

"But this is no poetry," he finally said. "'Tis true—the heat came at my own feet; yes! I knelt, and with my hands and knees I knew a warmth that before I knew only from fire." At this he jumped up, for he could not contain himself. He went on, "And now I see the source of such heat. As a blacksmith's oven rages, so the core of our island lights up and burns white—and I see how the plains warm and the mountains' caverns ring and the forests writhe, all in expectation!" He paused and searched for more, his chest heaving. But no more came.

"What does the island wait for?" The question was whispered by the smallest child, who had wrapped himself in his mother's cloak as his father cried out.

"Hush, my dear," his mother replied.

"No!" his father said. He looked down upon his son with a smile, and his piercing look was kind. "He must know as we all know. We wait with the island, and it groans for the day when its healing will be complete. It is no poetry that I speak; no, it will be accomplished—our hands will touch what is now only a vision. Even you, small one, must wait with that truth growing in your heart." A final smile reassured the frightened child, and he reached out his arms. The shepherd held his son the rest of the night until the fire burned itself into ashes; they were together, and they were silent.

So, over the course of Mossy's first 12 years, such stories were told in marketplaces, in open lanes, and over fires. Across Cab Nilres they opened weary eyes and made glad the mouths of old men; draped in the royal colors of dawn, women sang new songs at their looms, and their children marveled at the words; those upon the coasts no longer looked out upon the grey sea in despair but saw life in the sun-illumined green waves that rolled toward them.

And yet, the hope of many would not hold back the dark days to come.

# CHAPTER 5

---

# The Invasion

Listen with the people of Cab Nilres—hear the beat of wings, the cry and call of the birds of prey! From the three mountain peaks rose eagles into the air. The scent of battle stirred them from their nests, and with their focused gaze they searched the far shores. Again and again their voices pierced the air, for they were eager for the hunt. This is what those mighty birds witnessed.

At sea, ships of dark wood and dark sails moored and breathed fiery arrows over Point Bay, and the beach roared in flames from the assault. The king's men were forced to give way and took refuge within the forest nearby; they watched as boats filled with men and beasts were lowered from the multitude of ships and made ready. An unsteady quiet fell, only to be broken when the black army landed. Terrible banners snapped wildly and filled both sky and waves like a gathering storm.

Leagues away, back where the canyon divided the island, those at the great bridge prepared its defense. The king himself watched for news from one of the bridge's towers, and below, men obeyed his order to ready the bridge for its destruction—a final defense if needed. They stacked wood and heated oil at its four corners and prayed to never have to light it. At all this, the king grew faint at the thought of Sir Miles and the fate of all his knights.

He turned his face to the heavens and said, "Grant them victory and good speed."

The eagles also saw this: In the valley close to the castle, tents of solid color, of stripes, and of checks flapped in the breeze. It was a camp of solemn gathering made up of men and women from the castle and those from the farthest ends of Cab Nilres. The Week of Knights had begun despite the looming attack, yet the bonfires did not reach so high, and the music was only half played. All felt the fall of a murky night even though the sun blazed in its own blue tent.

The castle stood hushed. It also had been fortified, and its attendants looked on and awaited what all feared but refused to speak aloud.

A trumpet blast from the tallest tower of the bridge! It called in answer to the towers of the coast—for the dark horde landed amid the flaming brands, their horses and riders eager to break the island's calm.

From the vantage point of their flight, the sharp-eyed eagles watched the king's men hold their line within the trees. Even as the enemy raged up the beach, the good knights waited to strike.

How they clashed! How the lines collided! And arrows rained from the ships anew, igniting a great fire in the forest so hot and full of smoke, the battle was cut off from the eagles' sight.

The great birds drew back and circled the canyon and bridge. As the fire and battle on the coast spread, the king gave the order to pull back to the castle. Each corner of the bridge was checked and rechecked; at one command all would be lit to destroy the enemy's way across the canyon. In silence, with heads bowed, the servants of the king obeyed and left their posts. The only men of war to remain were four archers, armed with arrows and fire. They were to wait for any of Sir Miles's men to retreat before they set the bridge afire.

Only the sounds of clashing metal, heavy hoofbeats, and cries of attack rose from beyond the canyon, for the sights of war remained covered by the thick-standing aspen trees. A quaking fear mingled with the sounds, and the four archers spoke words to one another—words to defy their fear and remain steadfast.

And all at once the fighting burst into the open. A remnant of Sir Miles's men drew back as they fought bravely, but the enemy came on like an endless plague. Sir Miles himself heaved his massive war axe and pummeled every man and beast within its arc.

Lo! The blast of a trumpet! With reluctance and rage, the horde drew back. A silence fell. The knights of Cab Nilres became still, their exhaustion forcing them to remain. Did the enemy retreat?

Sir Miles turned and saw the bridge remained intact, the fires yet unlit. His frustration showed on his brow, for he wished then that all the bridge's wood was smoldering with its stones at the bottom of the canyon.

Another blast!

And with the trumpet call came the shout of the dark army. The ground shook, and the forest trembled.

"Make ready the flaming arrows!" Sir Miles called across the canyon, and the archers remembered their task.

Something approached, for the ground trembled anew and with gathering force until the bridge itself quaked.

Sir Miles spoke again, "Fall back to the threshold of the bridge! They will not take it." Quickly, his few knights settled into formation across the entrance. One by one Sir Miles looked into the eyes of his men; he did not speak, but all knew it was a final farewell. "For the redemption of Cab Nilres!" he cried, and his men repeated the centuries-old battle cry, "For the redemption of Cab Nilres!" Their feet felt the pounding of the earth, and they prepared their weapons for war and their souls for death.

Before another thought could pass through their minds, or another prayer could pass over their lips, the forest gave way to a massive beast that swung a gleaming horn and gnashed sharp teeth. When it beheld the bridge, it reared up and roared. Its rider gripped a bow and shot, felling not the knights barring the way, but two of the archers beyond the canyon.

Sir Miles turned and shouted to the two who remained, "Now! Set the fires now!" But only one heard, for the other had panicked and was consumed with fear. "Light it," Sir Miles ordered his men. "Go! Light it!" Immediately, four broke away and ran to the far side of the bridge.

The beast's cry ripped through the ears of the king's men, and Sir Miles charged to meet it. An arrow shot by the rider pierced his shoulder, but he raised his axe and aimed rightly. It seemed he meant to be trampled, but he brought a mighty stroke down upon the joint of a front leg. The beast swept its head to gore him and caught his side. The rider screamed and leapt away as the monster tripped from the axe-wound. Another cry from the enraged rider set the black horde in motion, and the knights of Cab Nilres rallied to Sir Miles's side.

Blood poured from his wounds, and his men feared for him, but he encouraged them. "To the bridge! Take heart, we will bring many with us to the grave. Cab Nilres will yet flourish!"

So it was that Sir Miles and his men took a final stand upon the bridge. From behind, the two remaining archers joined them; one begged forgiveness with burning cheeks, and he was counted among those who fell bravely that day.

Though the enemy surged onto the bridge, it would not be theirs. From the far end rose the heat and smoke of a fire that grew and exploded with the touch of hot oil. And it was too late for those of the black horde who had been drawn into the trap.

The fighting was at its fiercest when the great stones began to fall into the canyon. For a time this stirred up the king's knights to push deep into the enemy line; they knew their fate, and it drove them on. Yet, when Sir Miles felt the bridge quake and shudder, he gave the order to pull back to lure more of the dark army forward. In fury did the foe lunge and charge, a taste of victory on their lips—too late! A sickening crack of stone and wood! And in smoke and flame the bridge fell.

The canyon's depths rang with the clamor of men and the tumult of the massive structure as it crashed far below on rock and water. Smoke and steam mingled and shot into the sky—a sure signal to the whole of Cab Nilres that Sir Miles and his men gave all.

And who of the island, when considering these mighty men, does not now remember the oft-told story that so delighted Sir Miles? Yes, these words that passed his lips forever whisper their memorial, "to the end he and they were one." And, "The love they bore for one another drove them on, and though they scattered the evil foe, together all paid for victory with his last breath."

Flying from the canyon, wheeling above the castle walls, the eagles of the distant peaks witnessed the king and queen in their sorrow. They walked upon a high tower, the destruction of the bridge rising before them, and watched as ever more of the enemy's forces amassed beyond the canyon. They feared the days to come, and for Mossy they prayed and hoped.

That night, as if the heavens showed mercy from the clouds, a cool rain fell that extinguished the fires of battle and pattered on the castle walls to soothe the occupants—not the least of these was the king and queen, whose fears ate at their hope for Cab Nilres and for their son.

# CHAPTER 6

---

# Mossy's Travels

As you are sure to remember, we left Mossy by the secret lake, and we wondered what his three visions meant—and well we should, for he wondered the same. Yes, and after we left him, a call settled on his heart to think no more, but act. So he pushed himself up and hiked out of the steep valley.

The morning stars gave him light until rosy dawn shot into the sky. At a high place clear of forest growth, he turned east. The island was yet covered in shadow, but the mountain tops and wide horizon on the sea announced the day.

From where Mossy was he could just make out the canyon and valley close to his father's castle. The canyon stretched across the island like a thin ribbon of indigo silk, and the valley lay like the cup of an open palm. He watched until the sun bathed both in warm light.

Soon, a change came over the water. It was the black army, its ships uncountable. To him it looked like a second night, like shadows of darkness that refused to obey the sun. They came closer and closer as he watched. He stood still as a stone and could not turn away; the whole sea looked poisoned before him. He was divided, for a pang of longing brought the comforts of home to mind, and he remembered his choice to miss The Week of Knights. The rims of his eyes reddened and dropped tears upon the ground.

An eagle's cry shocked him out of his misery—he ducked, and the skin of his knee was ripped to the bone on the rock beneath it. He watched his blood and tears mix on the ground, and the ancient prophecy spoken through Lord Salix helped him endure the pain:

> *The word of his mouth*
> *Brings forth healing.*

Suddenly, he remembered the canyon. His wound and his tutor's words about the island's canyon-wound came together. His open and bleeding knee before him and the old story that worked upon his heart, both revealed a new vision to him—he saw the walls of the canyon filled with a bright orange light that intensified until the whole of it was hot white. It became a jolt of fire that shot into the sky, a thread spun into the wheel of dancing stars.

Mossy shook himself a moment later and grimaced at the pain. Blood and water gathered in a small pool by his hand. He swallowed his fear, rose to his full height in the morning light, and continued to climb into the mountain. Soon, he bowed his head as he hiked; his thoughts consumed him, and he did not mark the way. Indeed, not until he stood upon a distant peak did he look at his surroundings, for the tug within him guided his steps. The day passed.

Thick mists twirled and gathered around Mossy, and he no longer tried to see the isle below, but waited. Darkness came, and with it, sleep. He slept in the fog of meaningless dreams, and it seemed only a moment before he awoke wet with dew in the predawn morning.

He was not surprised to find he had slept at the mouth of a cave, from which poured a constant hiss of sound and steam, and it was clear to him then that he must search the island to its core. What he would find was a mystery he marveled at, but search he must.

Mossy knelt on the dew-soaked ground, and with his face and palms lifted up, he wove a prayer; it welled up in him and spilled out. The words coursed through him like water through a tree's trunk—and so it was that the prayer was fully his and also fully strange to him.

He looked upon daylight from the shelter of the cave's entrance before he knew he had risen and ceased to pray. "For the redemption of Cab Nilres," Mossy said. The words echoed though he spoke softly. He turned into the warm dark, and steam kissed his forehead.

Many songs have been made that sing of Mossy's travels through the caverns and deeps, and all the lays that describe his courage are sung rightly. However, those sung that describe monstrous forms fighting with him claw and tooth sing only of the battle that raged within him. For, until his search came nearly to an end, he traveled in darkness. But, my boys, do not think that this inner struggle was somehow less than a struggle fought with hands. No! It became for him a burden almost unbearable, a burden no mighty work of human hands could remove.

He descended slowly, for the weight he carried was heavy; his fingers sought out the way, and when he had gone on for what felt like many days, he crawled and then dragged himself on his belly. Wet from constant steam and sweat, bloodied from scrapes on unseen stones, pressed down from pain of heart, he cried out what he thought would be his final word, uttered with his final breath: "Mercy!"

And with the word cast out before him, he laid still, his forehead on rock and his hands open at his sides.

Immediately, a change in his surroundings caused him to look up. A red, glowing light the size of a closed fist danced in front of him. It flickered like sunlight reflected through leaves on the forest floor.

Mossy crawled to it and shed tears of hope, for it spread out before him as he approached. The way was farther down, but the sloped passage filled with dry brightness the longer he followed it. His pulse beat quickly, and his eyes were slow to adjust to the strong light, which forced him to stop for rest.

He did not know how long he rested, for he woke from sleep to find he walked within halls of ever-flashing light. He ran his fingers through the beams and points of light and marveled at the flickering walls, which were patterned with unending diamonds, and the way took him into yet deeper caverns, all filled with light. Soon, he knew, he would find the source and understand why it must be so.

Again it was like he slept and woke.

Immediately, he heard a roar of great volume, and he found that he stood close to a flowing river of fire. The gallery walls surrounding him glowed white, but he remained in the midst of it without pain. His eyes and ears were fully opened, and no longer did his burden weigh upon his shoulders. In the midst of the roar he was reminded of many things: the mystery of his childhood dream that swept over him so often, the visions by the secret lake, and the joy and connection he felt with his tutor and friend Lord Salix. And yet the greatest memory that now flooded over him was the simple image of the One who came to him with the burning coal; his eyes of bronze smoldered deeply into Mossy again.

He would have fed upon his memories for countless moments, but a new sound came from the river. First a bubbling, then a rolling, splashing noise. Mossy saw massive shapes in the rolling flames, and the whole of all he could see came to life. Liquid fire shot and spurted up and around him, and the roar increased. Great numbers of rock—burning and smoking—fell and broke before the shore until Mossy thought the mountain itself was collapsing.

However, just when noise and fire made their most dangerous outburst, so Mossy thought, a silence fell. The river all but stopped. Mossy fixed his attention upon a black rock in the fire. It alone moved—no! How could it be? It grew and the flames slid off its sides, for it rose out of the depths and settled onto the shore.

The rock, which was black as a moonless night, took a form— from a shapeless mass it lengthened and stretched into a head and body like a horse. It shook its tremendous mane, and the ground and cave walls trembled at its first terrible neigh. Fire dripped from its belly and fell off its sides as it walked to Mossy; smoke billowed from its nose with every breath.

At Mossy's touch, the living rock did not pull away but pressed its giant muzzle into his hand. It stomped, and Mossy thought of the chargers of his father's stables, those gallant steeds trained for war or jousting—impatient and eager for the clash of battle. And of course, he now knew, his dream of old had prepared him for this meeting.

Mossy spoke to the beast, and his mind turned over this new and wonderful thing; he was hushed and became still when the head of the rock-animal bowed and its body stooped. Quickly, he climbed onto its back.

Welling up from inside, words flowed into him once more, and with every stomp from his new-made horse, the urge to cry out grew. He raised his hands and shouted until he had no more breath.

The cavern rumbled. Mossy looked to the river as the sound increased. Until the whole of the fire-river turned black, rock shapes emerged and formed themselves as the first rock creature had done. Mossy could not count them—and the liquid flames produced more and more. He raised his hands again and these words erupted from his mouth, "For the redemption of Cab Nilres!"

# CHAPTER 7

## The Island Moves

Deep within the island Mossy's shout echoed, and how can we not be glad at his discovery? Mossy has helped us understand the urgent sounds of the caverns and the heat of the island's foundation—and soon the whole of Cab Nilres will know as well. And yet, there is more to be told of those who follow Lord Salix, more of the expectation of the trees.

What did the hermit say of the forest but that it moved as one on Mossy's name-day, and that "the giants shook and their roots crawled as if to release themselves from bondage"? What more could we hear to add to our own expectation?

But there is more.

Mossy grew and the trees watched him with their slow and deliberate eagerness; he walked with Lord Salix, and they knew what was to come; the night on the secret shore finally arrived, and the ancient ones sent a company to greet him. These things we know.

Yet this is new:

As Mossy sped from the valley that housed the secret lake, even as he climbed the steep heights and explored the bowels of Cab Nilres, Lord Salix and his host made themselves ready.

The multitude of interlocking fingertips that stretch under all the ground of the island—the network of trees and shrubs made up of friendly roots—spoke through a steady pulse. So steady, in fact, that it resembled the beat of a human heart.

It communicated Mossy's decision and travels and foretold what was to come—but mixed with joyful news were two somber truths: the tears of Mossy's mother-queen soaked the forest floor, and the island crawled with evil.

As the whole of the island's forest knew, the queen looked for a moment to shed tears that only a mother could cry; she stood on the boundary of the castle's garden and faced the moonless night. And though the light from the stars glowed pale and soft, her cheeks glistened. She wept there, alone, the fallen leaves her only companions.

But what fine companions! For what are leaves but the messengers of trees? The queen desired her sorrow to be hidden there in the privacy of the garden, but each tear was a silent treasure, first for the dry leaves, and second for the very ground. Quickly, her liquid misery spread under Cab Nilres, and all that possessed roots mourned with her.

This, then, is how the music began.

High on the blusterous cliffs of Mount Clarus, where contorted stems of willows cling to sharp precipices, a lady of arboreal beauty rose from a twisted trunk. She had drunk long of the queen's tears, and sorrow was not unknown to her.

From the sheer side of the mountain the willow-lady sang her lament. Through narrow halls of rock her song grew and echoed until it reached the castle garden. So it was that the queen heard a new, strange song that somehow touched a familiar chord. She thought her own mind made the words, and this is true, but soon she knew her longing for Mossy was not hers alone. Indeed, her tears dropped all the more, and in a flash she knew the connection they made with the island. She raised her voice in harmony with the lament coming from the mountain, and in this her hope and resolve were restored.

The whole gathered congregation of Cab Nilres would also hear the willow's song, and together be moved as their queen was moved—yet the trees were stirred for the sake of their anger as well.

Below the canyon, the giant army swarmed in its restless desire to crush the island. One defeat blinded the host and its leaders with naked rage that spread over the beaches and into wooded paths. The forest felt the roll of advancing war machines and the stomp of numberless soldiers.

It would not be long before the foe covered the entire island, and the roots pulsed with indignation at what their enemy sought: to further curse the ground with shame. On and on the pulse beat, and the growing things prepared themselves for action.

# CHAPTER 8

# In the Presence of Their Enemies

B ack in the castle-home of the king and queen, a tumult of voices rang within the court as each word of counsel was debated. The knights who were left ached to have their turn in battle, and many of them cared not whether they met death. Said one of the men to the king, "My lord, I've seen the war-constructions of the black army. They intend to build many of their own bridges to cross the canyon. Give the order, my lord, and we shall rain fire upon them."

And the king, who loved his fighting knights, looked thankfully upon the one who spoke, and said, "Good knight, steady the hands of your men. Soon you will all act, and waiting will end. Hold fast and pray."

Others spoke this counsel, "My king, the mountain at our back contains many caves. Let us prepare for retreat—especially for the old, the new mothers, and the children."

The king returned this answer, "What you say is full of kindness. Yet I fear we would be overtaken with no refuge. The ways are hard—both steep and rocky. Many would perish on the way." The king paused and let silence fill the court. He looked upon everyone gathered, and then he opened his mouth and said:

"Another counsel I have received. This word places me among the rocks that the waves of the sea continually batter. Even so, it is the way we must take. Hear, all of you, what I say.

"The prophecies of old tell that these days of evil were to come; I know of no other evil that is greater than the foe beyond the canyon. It is said the island itself will rise up to our aid—through one of us. Is it not so? The wise through the ages have told that the trees sway in the wind that whispers it, that the hollows and caverns echo what has been etched from times before our time, that the rocks of this isle rest upon a foundation laid with this truth."

At this, the people of the court murmured and spoke with divided minds, for some held these things as foolish tales, while others told of their tingling ears at such words.

"Please," said the king, and he raised his hand for all to be quiet. "This is my decree: In the presence of our enemies, we carry on with The Week of Knights. And this will be the new treasure brought out with the old—with our play and festivity, the one who will defeat the foe will be revealed."

Once the king had made his decree, no further counsel was given, and the people departed—though many were still divided. So it was that some hoped beyond all hope, even in the midst of those whose hearts remained hard.

The king gave orders for all to be prepared, and when he was alone with his queen, he showed his secret anguish. Together they mourned over their personal loss and the plight of their people, too.

Wiping the king's tears away, she said, "You spoke well, and you must stand in the midst of the festival. Show yourself in the gathering, in the shadow of our enemies, and we, too, shall hold fast and pray."

The king and queen, and all the court, assembled in the valley that day. Much music and dance began at their arrival, and the king proclaimed their feasting should begin in honor of the fallen.

Said the king, "Those who cut off the enemy's advance did so with valor. We remember their deeds. This Week of Knights will be like no other. With danger at our front door, we rejoice that our salvation will come to us as it has been told. And this I ask of all, that tonight as the bonfires reach their fingers to heaven, that we, too, will offer our prayers of faith."

Those within the crowd knew that Mossy was still gone, and many close to the king saw the evidence on his face. In this way, his presence and words uplifted them, for he showed himself as one of their own, as one who knew loss and sorrow. And even though some doubted, all responded so the whole valley rang, and those beyond the canyon heard this: "For the redemption of Cab Nilres!" The trees of the fields clapped their hands, and their noise startled the whole assembly. Wonder fell upon them—in a great silence they stood and waited, for there was no wind. How then had the branches tossed and the leaves waved? Though the question rose inside everyone, none dared ask it aloud.

Finally, the king gave his trumpeter the order to usher in the feasting, for the games would not begin until the sun's rising the following day. Therefore tables were set, fires were stoked in the stone ovens, and the smell of roasted venison filled the camp and beyond.

With an open hand, the king urged the servants of his court to help the people—"May they lose themselves in what should be joy to them! Have faith and show it in this: we shall carry on even as our enemy bangs on the door—may it be salve to our hearts and a sign of defeat to our foe!" And with many other words he blessed them and bade them do as he asked.

So saying, he threw off his own sorrow and greeted the young boys who were to compete in the games, giving special honor to those who had lost father, brother, uncle, or grandfather in the first days of battle. He also instructed them on the contests ahead, and as evening came, and those who surrounded him were flanked both by shadows and the light of many fires, he fancied he saw his own son. A familiar gesture or smile, the shape of a cheekbone or hairline, a toss of hand or arm caught fleetingly in the corner of his eye made him believe for a flash of a moment that Mossy was near. By and by, the cover of night settled on the island, and he grew quiet and pensive.

Was it so long ago that he watched Mossy climb the old wil-low in their courtyard? He allowed the image of his son's smile to form in his mind, and he could hear the wispy sweep of weeping branches—or was that the sound he heard now beyond the fire-light? At the king's side, the grey-eyed dreamer smiled and nod-ded. His presence was welcome, and the king recalled the peace of his word: Mossy will return. Have faith.

Music played. Try as they might, the musicians could not keep the tunes quick and joyful for long but fell in with the mood of thought around them. Again and again it was marked by the entire host of those gathered that the wind held its breath—and yet the branches of the trees tossed as long as there was music, and in the morning, when sunlight dissolved night's cover, they did not forget it.

Yes, with the first light of morning, and before the weight of danger became too heavy to bear, a song filled the camp. A lone harp matched a lone voice. It was the willow-lady of the mountain, the same singer who took up the queen's tearful lament. She trav-eled long to lift the song once again, yet now, as the queen heard for herself, she also mixed it with a deeper sorrow.

Instinctively, the entire company circled the one who sang the mournful melody. The king, too, came and listened so his ears tingled. Those standing near him saw wonder in his eyes, and it caused them to be caught up in further awe.

The lady did not hide her nature. Her harp was shaped from her hair, which was a mass of string-like branches. Her arms were the color of willow bark, mottled brown and green. Her voice—ah! Her voice sounded as though she swept her hair over a clear stream, her leaflets dancing in the shallows.

Now the people understood how the trees moved of their own accord, for here it was revealed to them. Therefore they lis-tened all the more attentively.

Soon, they all remembered the music from some deep memory, but perceived the song was new. Somehow their inmost selves had been waiting for these words to be sung from their first breaths. The song hung in the air long after the last note, long after the singer had departed—and none knew where she had come from or where she had gone. For moments uncounted the people stood silently; side by side, each was alone with private thoughts that stirred their blood. And even as they moved about once more, the chords echoed through the halls of their minds.

On the other side of the canyon, the enemy raged. They raged because of the feasting the night before and because of the singing at dawn's breaking. These things stopped the spell of fear they tried to cast and birthed their own fear—for it was clear to the black army that the trees were on the move, and that not only the music moved them, but hostility also. As they had attempted to build makeshift bridges to span the canyon, many of their men had begun to cut down timber on the edge of an open clearing. Directly afterward, they found themselves surrounded, both unable and unwilling to swing their axes because of the dense undergrowth that surged at them.

And so they kindled fire, yet this also proved a failure. Night and day wrought a dew from the ground that muffled the flames before they grew hot. Smoke stung their eyes; brambles and thorns held fast to their pale skin. Their animals, too, became restless and fought with the handlers. Many times the great horned beasts broke free of their bonds and gave vent to their blind anger born of fear.

In spite of all this, the enemy readied its attack. The ships anchored in the bay held more men and siege works than seemed possible, and wave after wave of black banners had suffocated the beach. Their first battle tactic averted, they meant to blot out the whole of the island with sheer numbers.

Even so, The Week of Knights proceeded. With the willow-lady's song fresh within them all, they spoke well of one another to spur themselves toward victory. For, even with the dark evil brooding close by, they knew it approached—a victory planned for them before mankind stepped foot on the isle.

When the sun's rays announced mid-morning, the games of The Week began. It had been decided that The Week should be shortened, therefore the games were played quickly on one day and with the final contest always in sight. All became more and more aware of the growing noise across the canyon, but they resolved to carry on with more vigor—for, they said to one another, perhaps these contests will show who will save us. Knights both old and young, along with all who looked on or played a harp or lyre, took note that the king had a new counselor: a grey-eyed man from the distant western coast. Some remembered his presence at court, and that he had talked of Mossy.

In the course of time, all the games but one had been played. And so, in their turns, the young knights-to-be tested themselves with the final contest of hand-to-hand combat. Each contestant fought father, older brother, or uncle, and one by one they came to the center to win and be welcomed a knight, or lose and return to boyhood.

Until the sun turned toward evening, boys came and showed they were worthy to enter the king's service as a man—and a good many waited with anticipation for the end of the day when the king would knight them all.

As for the king himself, his heart was mixed with joy and sorrow both. Joy for those who stood up under the tests that day, and sorrow at two things: that they would soon meet an evil foe, and that Mossy was not among them.

And yet, the word spoken to him was also twofold. Though she melted within, the queen smiled upon him and said, "Hold fast." And her clear eyes told the story of her own woe. His new counselor, the old one at his other hand, spoke this way, "When you complete the games and knight these new-made men, stand and face the mountain to the west. Have faith." And his own faith grew stronger at his exhortation.

All continued to marvel at the courage of their own people, and, indeed, as the day wore on and the young men waited for their king to knight them, the whole body of those gathered was strengthened. And it came to pass that the queen, too, rose up when her husband stepped into the circle of knights and knights-to-be; she walked among the people with a steady hand and straight back, and it was quickly noticed that she carried dagger, bow, and arrows. It was then the mothers and sisters of the island rose up with one accord to join their queen. Let it be recorded: many of the pale-faced enemies were loath that day to come upon the women of Cab Nilres, for their loyalty kindled a hot fire within that became wrath not easily quenched.

And so, at the fullness of time, the king attended the young men within the ring of contest. All waited for him to unsheathe his sword and begin; instead he removed his outer, heavy garments and laid aside his weapon. He looked at his hands as he clenched and unclenched them. Finally, he turned his back to the young men and fixed his attention on the western heights.

No one dared speak. Silence descended on the camp so the pop of low-burning fires became loud to their ears, and all stilled their feet.

"Men and women of Cab Nilres!" The king's voice was like thunder to them, sudden and splitting. "I am in need." Again, an astonished hush fell, and it was a weight on every neck to bear it. "I am in need of your prayers to stand here in faith and believe what is now unseen. Come to my aid!"

Stillness settled in their marrow. Many heartbeats later, all watched their king bow his head and lift his hands. A single, soft breeze came through the people then, and each man and woman thought they heard the prayer of those standing near: "May the fruit of his sorrow be joy." Yet no lips uttered that initial prayer. Indeed, the breeze died, and the trees again tossed of their own power.

It was then that every head bowed.

Was it long that they prayed? None knew. It wasn't until the ground shook that they opened their eyes. The king, too, looked for what was surely a mighty storm descending from the mountains, but not even one cloud could he find—only the deep blue sky of a dying afternoon. Awe overcame the whole assembly so when a scout ran in among them, he had to shout many times before anyone heard him. "Thick blackness falls from the mountainside—flashes of fire and bursts of smoke go before it. Take cover!" And if the shaking had not ceased and the source not made itself clear, the people would have fled, for many thought the black army had crossed the canyon and were falling on them from all sides.

But the king lifted his voice and said, "Hold!" For he had seen the line of smoke and fire halt at the rim of the valley. He watched. Hope budded in him as a swift rider broke away from the dark confusion. At an impossible speed, much faster than any horse's legs can run, he came toward the camp—and even so, his appearance became clear as he rode, and the king knew him.

Now the hope newly opened in the king blossomed and grew into the fruit of joy. How he wanted to shout and embrace his lost son! How he longed to welcome his boy back from the unknown— no, he felt more, as though he were back from the dead!

The queen came to his side and took his hand in hers. They smiled at one another yet dared not speak. The king saw in her the same joy, the same desire to welcome Mossy with open relief. Standing together to see how Mossy had been changed, their new hope was that their son had become what all the island had waited for, all that they needed.

The people, however, beheld a youth with glowing bronze eyes, who rode upon a beast larger than their fears. It breathed fire as it ran. It passed through the crowd and halted in the midst of them so suddenly that none thought to hide or cover themselves. Before they caught their breath, the terrible presence of horse and rider stood opposite the king—the queen herself encouraging her husband forward!

And then they watched the rider dismount and remove his outer cloak. He approached the king, and no one sought to stop the newcomer, for to them it was like a dream in which they could only watch.

Of course, it was like a dream to the king and Mossy, too. How was it that father and son did not fall upon one another's necks and cry tears of joy at their reunion? It was because they had yearned for the moment they would lay hands on one another at the conclusion of The Week of Knights. So, in the midst of the congregation, and in the presence of a mighty enemy, father and son fought their battle. And as was the custom, as soon as the king knew the strength of Mossy—indeed, as soon as he was assured that his son was now a young man—he relented, and it was his great joy to present Mossy as the first of his newest knights.

For their part, the people were slow to understand that Mossy had returned. The shock of the way he returned, on the back of his rock-beast amid a firestorm, had clouded their minds. But when the king received him and the combat began, they saw him for who he was. Many looked to his mother-queen, and her tears confirmed the prince's return. They were as the songs say: clear as a swiftly running stream—the refreshment sought after by so many whose thirst felt unquenchable.

A voice boomed through the camp and stopped the congregation's reveries. "Behold! My son! The future king of Cab Nilres!" And with many other words the king rejoiced. The entire camp echoed his gladness, and they watched how he could not take his eyes off Mossy as he knighted the other young men.

When it was finished, a new company of knights stood before the people, and for a short time music and good tidings prevailed.

# CHAPTER 9

## The Charge

Did we not celebrate when Mossy became his father's knight? Did we not desire along with him that The Week would bring him into manhood—indeed, into the arms of adventure? Yes! And more! Our ears yearn to hear his story further told. Listen!

In the fullness of time the entire camp heard Mossy's voice. He remounted the massive creature that now stomped impatiently, and he said, "Today, Cab Nilres is fully vindicated! Let no one shrink back or be dismayed. I witnessed this onyx-colored beast rise from the fiery liquid within the heart of the island. It is not to be feared. More of the rock-horses wait at the entrance of the valley to gain riders; when they enter our camp, they will make clear who is chosen to ride. Those who remain: comfort the weak, and prepare to welcome back any who are wounded, for there will be many."

The king looked on as his son gave wise orders; it was a glad sight to watch as Mossy proved himself ready. He would have lifted his voice to stir the people up on Mossy's behalf, but at that moment the earth quaked.

So terrible was the sound and so overwhelming the sight, that even though Mossy had told them what was to come, many hid themselves. Any who remained divided at heart could not stand what looked to them a rockslide of the entire mountain.

But the eyes of others were opened, and they saw that down the valley stormed a mighty wave of war horses. Their manes smoked and their hooves burned coal-like. The tumult of their charge filled the valley, and it did not cease until the last horse halted and the echoes died a booming death. A countless number waited for worthy riders, and men and women alike stepped to their rock-horses and mounted.

Immediately a crack from the forest rent the air. Many sounds followed, like many branches splitting in two. Was it a dream? Or did the valley empty itself of its trees as though to drain them in the canyon?

But no one had time to gather an answer, for Mossy lifted his voice and his newly-got blade. The chargers forged in the ovens of the earth's core answered Mossy with a war cry of their own; it went before them like an awful gale.

The trees leading the charge, the young cavalry rode down the length of the valley and sighted the canyon. The horses pounded the ground and covered it completely. Not one rider thought of how they would cross the canyon until they saw it fully, and even with the question rising in their minds, the massive creatures' fury and speed doubled.

All of a sudden the host of them entered a kind of avenue—the trees from the valley had arranged themselves so—and the beasts' nostrils smoked and flamed. The branches pointed the way and spurred them on. Sound of hooves and sound of clashing weaponry increased to a wild pitch within the hall of trees; the noise preceded the cavalry's arrival and was its own kind of weapon.

The edge of the canyon drew near! Would they leap such an impossible width? But what bridge was this? Out from the cliffs were sturdy rods of wood that spanned the gap before the riders—what was it? Mossy understood immediately, but none other knew until they watched him charge across. Hundreds of trees lined the rim along both sides of the canyon, and they had shot their roots over the expanse to form a bridge. And more! Once the canyon was behind them, they saw that a great space opened before them.

A way had been made to a flat battleground where the bewildered enemy camped.

War horns sounded, but it was too late. What army could withstand an assault from every growing thing, or fight against the offspring of the mountains? Rage from the riders, too, fell heavily upon them, and the war machines, the single-horned animals, and those bearing swords and spears were crushed.

The first charge quickly ended, but Mossy pressed on, pursuing survivors on and on toward the ocean. All the rest spread out behind him and swept the remainder of the island. Across the tableland toward the Great Southern Cliffs, toward Connatus and Gemellus, they rushed to clean the whole of Cab Nilres—but Mossy and his noble parents, along with the entirety of the newest knights, made straight for the Bay of Aecor. The trees had parted, and to those riding the towering cottonwoods bowed as they passed through.

Black banners quickly came into view, but the sight of the enemy served only to fuel the war-passions of horses and riders alike, for they sped on and their foes trembled at the sound.

The clash was mighty at the beachhead. Battle-hardened infantry, both huge and heavily armored, met Mossy's charge and did not flee or hesitate. Even so, the flash of tempered steel and streams of fire from the horses' mouths pushed them back. Boats full of reinforcements saw the fury of the charge and turned back toward the galleons beyond the breakers. From the large ships, Mossy's attack looked like an eruption which poured out both lava and fierce warriors. While the fighting grew hot on the beach, the black sails unfurled upon the wind—a sure sign of their retreat.

Those of the black army who fought on the island realized that their escape was cut off, and a howl of hate pierced the sky. The commanders in the boats approaching the fight ignored their cries. Fear of Mossy and the chargers' rage caused them to turn back toward the black ships, leaving the remnant in Mossy's hands. Yet the infantry on the shore redoubled their will to fight.

This is how all was ended:

Once the brave women-fighters saw both the ships and boats turn to retreat, they urged their charcoal horses to the Rock of Impeto, which towered above the bay. Without delay they formed ranks and filled the rowing boats with fiery arrows. The soldiers who were not struck took to the sea for refuge but found instead a watery grave.

A sharp and fearful pang filled the archers when they watched the warships turn to escape, for though their arrows found the boats easily, none could reach the ships. The queen clutched her bow with white knuckles, for the thought seized her that if this evil were not snuffed out completely, it would return tenfold upon others or upon Cab Nilres. And her thought was as true as every arrow shot from her bow.

But a murmur ran through the women on the rock, for across the bay, on the twin point Impetus that thrusts its towering head farther out to sea, a walking spinney of willows cast their string-like branches upon the cliffs. When the trees did this, loud noises echoed around the bay, for the willows tore chunks out of the cliff wall. A moment more and the trees spun as though a hurricane wind fell upon them, so great was their confusion. Yet, as the new-torn rocks flew toward the retreating galleons beyond the breaking waves, a pattern like a wild dance showed itself. More trees joined in until the spinney became a full forest stand, all hurling, flinging rock-missiles upon the enemy.

What then should the archers watch? The wild, tossing waltz? Or the outcome of their raucous play? Great was their rejoicing at the sight of the dance, and yet, as the ships took on the stones that rained upon them, their joy was renewed as each black ship broke apart and sank. And here, where the trees showed their mettle, the singing willow-lady looked upon the queen. Though the bay was between them, they knew one another, their understanding complete.

All the while, Mossy and his cavalry pushed the enraged black army into the sea. More and more of the foe perished, but this only caused the evil soldiers left to go berserk. In their blind anger they spent themselves fighting the rock horses of Cab Nilres, which was like fighting the heart of the island itself. Finally, the last handful of the enemy pulled back, for they knew their defeat.

Mossy drew up his mount, and his own wrath, too, had to be restrained as he spoke like one who knew the touch of mercy. "Relent! Throw your weapons to the waves. We will give quarter." And he held out his hand to them. But let it be told now, so you who hear may understand, the enemy heard Mossy's voice and turned from his mercy. One by one they walked into the waters and let their heavy gear drag them to the rocky depths. Again, let it be known, they forsook the kindness offered, and their graves swallowed them.

Silence gripped those of Cab Nilres as the sounds of battle faded and were replaced with the endless rise and fall of the sea; they quaked at the thought of a darkness so dark that it could spurn mercy and welcome cold death—and even the bravest of the knights shuddered though the air blew warmly over their brows.

But only for a moment did they remain quiet, for victory was theirs. The shout that went up at the defeat of the black army resounded upon the cliffs of the bay—even as high as both points of rock: there! where the willows danced, and there! where the archers cheered! The riders slid to the sand and greeted one another in joy. Greatest, however, was the gladness and awe within the king, who watched his son move about the knights not as a boy, but as a man. And father and son also embraced, the gentle surf splashing at their feet.

# CHAPTER 10

# The Redemption of Cab Nilres

Now, my boys, listen as I recount to you the final chapter of this small story—of this Mossy story. For, as I have hinted, the people of the island were not alone in their desire for the full healing of Cab Nilres. And this is how the island became new:

Once the men upon the beach and the women upon the cliffs had briefly tasted victory, the horses blew bursts of impatient fire and nudged their riders, for the day was not yet done. Immediately, they found themselves once again charging, Mossy in the lead, and their jet black beasts surging with purpose back up the isle's slopes.

Did they dream? Or did the forest sing songs in step with their ascent? The melody came from the deepest parts of the way, where the moss grew thick in year-round coolness and shelter—hidden in leaves during winter and shrouded by thick-armed poplars during summer. The song produced clear images in each rider's imagination. They saw the canyon, black and bare and newly ripped open in the midst of constant flashes of lightning. And lo! A new sight! For the island's wound began to close and heal.

The pounding of rock-hooves snapped the reverie, and all wondered whether the song was first sung as they raced toward the canyon, or if it had always flowed from the forest—their ears finally hearing what Cab Nilres sang continually in secret song.

And Mossy was reminded of days gone by, of swaying branches in his parents' garden, of nights spent learning the throbbing language of the roots. How he had struggled to express what he learned! If the words had come rightly from his lips, would it have been anything other than this charge through the music of the deepest wood? This charge on the backs of hardened, living fire to the completion of the isle's redemption? He marveled at all that had passed and at the hint of what was to come.

For just as suddenly as the knights and fighting people woke from their dream of the canyon, behold! The horses stopped in front of the opening itself, and all looked upon the terrible wound as if for the first time. At some places, the smoldering remains of the bridge were visible, and once again the memory of those lost brought tears to the onlookers.

Their grief had no time to grow, however, for they all dismounted at a new wonder: the living rocks they sat upon grew unbearably hot, and their horse forms became blurred due to the waves of heat that pushed the people away. Smoke and flashes of fire mingled with the air. Great and awful cracks rose up, like a chorus of groaning boulders. Their ears rang at the sounds, and many fell to the ground in agony. For mercy, the cry of the rocks finally ended.

In the following dead silence, all of Cab Nilres's forces—men and women—were witness to the end and new beginning of their mounts. The horses' final charge came quickly, when no one looked for it. As one body they dove into the canyon, that constant reminder of the island's curse, and created a wall of ash and dust, which became the apostles of their mighty acts sent up and seen for miles. Its blast of heat and pressure pushed the people farther back, and for untold minutes the sky darkened. Heavy clouds swept in to double the artificial twilight, and a soft rain fell.

The heat and ash cleared and gave way to wisps of fog. Mossy stepped toward the canyon but did not find it; instead, he walked over smooth black stone like one might find at the bottom of a swift river. Those who watched him became poets that day, and what do their songs recount? Songs of his tears falling on the new-made ground—tears both of sorrow and joy; songs of the island moving on his behalf one last time to raise up a horse of flesh out of the dust that had settled on their feet; songs of this horse and its dark grey coat, the color of clouds full of rain and the color of ash mingled with tears; songs of how he greeted the animal and rode it to the source of the canyon-river to be made; songs of all the people running on feet that did not grow weary, for they yearned to follow Mossy.

And those poets sang well and rightly.

Mossy rode to the Great Southern Cliffs, to the feet of Mount Connatus and Mount Gemellus. Where these two meet, a black boulder had risen. Mossy said, "May this be forever a memorial of those who fell, and of the gift of Cab Nilres given once again to us." He drew his sword, lifted it over his head, and continued, "Let the island's healing be completed!" And he smote the stone so it broke and brought forth water. Yes, this is the spring that bubbles and flows to this day, the very source of the clear river that runs across the island in place of the canyon. Its water makes glad the valleys of the island, and the rock that is its bed reminds those who look on it of Mossy and their home's redemption.

The host of men and women then followed Mossy and his father and mother back to their castle-home. As they walked along the young river, their mouths filled with joyful song:

> *Let the trees of the island clap their hands!*
> *Let the sea billows roar its glad response!*
> *Make loud music to our God!*
> *For his foes have perished at his hand!*
> *Yes, the trees and the sea sing for joy,*
> *And the island has risen up for us—*
> *The foe was struck down utterly!*

Yes, and when the people lifted up their voices to praise and thank the Lord of All, they beheld the company of massive men and women Mossy met within the secret valley. Their forms suggested those of people, but the trees did not hide their true essence—for leaves burst forth and laughed upon the air, and the sky filled quickly with branches that played lutes and harps made of willow hair.

The king and queen, too, watched as Lord Salix walked alongside Mossy and his horse. Music and thanksgiving rang from their hearts. They held onto the moment and to one another, their hope completed.

The queen said, "The future king."

"Behold, my son," said his father. "He is Mossy."

Great was the festal gathering that night in the valley that had held The Week of Knights. The whole of the island rejoiced in their salvation and in the hopeful vision of their future, which lived in Mossy and was right in front of them and their children.

What more can be said about Mossy except that he became the king of Cab Nilres, and that he ruled with justice in his right hand and mercy in his left? The Week of Knights was celebrated year after year, giving the island new young men to serve the kingdom and guard against evil, all at the special encouragement of Mossy himself.

Mossy and his queen-wife, Laeta, noble daughter of Sir Miles, raised children of their own as well. They raised three boys who craved to test themselves against their father—and who were set aflame at two tales: of the old story passed down by Sir Miles himself, and of their grandfather's victory at The Battle of The Canyon-Bridge. How often those boys asked for the twin adventures, the one directly after the other, and how closely they followed each word! Long summer nights found them with their father in the garden, all three full of expectation, their faces glowing—a certain ancient tree dancing at the boys' delight.

Yes, and the wisdom of Lord Salix often guided Mossy, for the weeping willow remained long after the days of battle and redemption. From the First One's mouth came words in memoriam as well—words that some call poetry—for those who fell and for that which should not be forgotten.

And though Mossy became happy in his court, he at times sought out the solace of the forest. It was during those times that the depths of the woods called to him as they did when he was but a child, and he would walk along the memorial river that was once the canyon-wound of Cab Nilres. With one hand on the grey flank of his faithful horse, the water often led him into glens and open ways undisturbed and hidden from the commonly used roads. And it was there he knew again the wind in the branches of the cottonwoods and willows—just as he did when he was but three years old, his heart as full as ever. He remembered how he learned the ways of the forest in his father's garden, and he stood with closed eyes and uplifted arms to sway like he'd seen and heard them sway: back and forth, back and forth in step with the dance of heaven.